Peter Rabbit™

FOOTBALL FEVER!

D0336188

PUFFIN

Map of my woods

This is a map of the woods where I live. You can see who else lives here too. It's in my dad's journal which I always have with me.

ROCKY ISLAND

Old Brown is very bad tempered. We stay away from him.

OLD BROWN'S ISLAND

MR JEREMY FISHER'S POND

SQUIRREL NUTKIN'S WOOD

MRS TIGGY-WINKLE'S LAUNDRY

Squirrel Nutkin has some of the best, and nuttiest, ideas.

Squirrel Tribe – Nutkin's team of cheeky squirrel friends.

Flopsy and Mopsy the goody-goody twins are my older sisters.

JEMIMA PUDDLE-DUCK'S HILLTOP FARM

MR McGREGOR'S GARDEN

My friend, **Lily Bobtail.** Whatever the problem, she's got the answer.

MR TOD & TOMMY BROCK'S WOOD

MY BURROW

DR & MRS BOBTAIL'S BURROW

TUNNEL NETWORK

MR BOUNCER'S BURROW (BENJAMIN'S HOME)

RAVINE

DEEP DARK WOODS

DANDELION FIELD

Benjamin Bunny is my cousin. Whatever I do, he's right behind me – usually hiding!

One sunny day, Peter, Lily and Benjamin were playing football.

"To you, Lily!" shouted Peter.

But Peter kicked the acorn football too hard and it sailed high up into the trees . . .

"Ouch!" called a voice
and Nutkin appeared, rubbing his head.

"You clumsy rabbits should be
more careful!" Nutkin said.

"We're not clumsy," Peter replied crossly.

"Yes, you are," Nutkin said. "Squirrels are better than rabbits at EVERYTHING, especially nutball."

"Football!"

Benjamin laughed.

"That's what I said," Nutkin replied.

"We challenge you to a game!" said Peter.

"Rabbits versus squirrels. We'll soon show you who's best."

"You're on!" replied Nutkin. "Meet you here at 3 o'clock."

"Come on!" Peter shouted.
"Keep practising those passes."

"Practice makes perfect,"
said Lily.
"I know that for a fact."

"Do you really think we NEED to practise?" Benjamin panted. "I bet those silly squirrels don't even know the rules!"

"Let's pay them a visit and see," Peter suggested.

The rabbits found the squirrels
practising . . . sort of.

"Hey! Stop eating the balls!" Nutkin called,
as his squirrel team threw hazelnuts at each other.

Then Nutkin kicked a nut and . . . bonk, tap, kick –
the squirrels skilfully passed it around.

"We're ready!" Nutkin cheered.

"We're in trouble!"
Benjamin groaned.

It was time for the game to begin.
Nutkin had brought an extra-large
hazelnut to use as a ball.

Peter's sisters Flopsy and Mopsy had joined the rabbit team. They'd all been practising hard, but were still very nervous.

"We CAN'T lose this game!" Peter said.
"Nutkin will NEVER let us forget it!"

Peter kicked off and passed to
Flopsy . . . But a speedy squirrel
striker nipped in and took the ball,
racing towards the goal . . .

. . . as a black shadow fell across the pitch.

Old Brown swooped down with
a wicked gleam in his eye, as the
football players all dived for cover.

"That's MY hazelnut!"

Old Brown boomed at Nutkin.

"You stole it! I'm going to get it back, and then I'm going to get YOU!"

"This is very bad. This is very bad with an extra helping of uh-oh!" said Benjamin.

"HELP!" cried Nutkin, dodging here and there trying to escape from the angry owl.

The other squirrels ran around wildly, kicking acorns to distract Old Brown.

"We've got to help!" Peter cried.

"But how?" Lily asked.

"By working as a team," Peter said.

"Let's hop to it!"

"Nutkin, pass the ball to Benjamin!" Peter cried.

Nutkin kicked the hazelnut ball, and Old Brown turned to dive after it.

Benjamin quickly booted the ball
to Lily, who sprang forward and
headed it on to Peter.

Peter waited until the last second, then he leaped high
and kicked the ball hard – **GOAL!**

Old Brown turned sharply, following the ball . . .
and flew through the goal and straight into a
hollow tree trunk behind it!

"Tail feathers!"
squawked the befuddled bird.

At last, Old Brown managed to pull his head out of the hollow trunk. The grumpy owl flew away, with a sore head and NO nut.

"HOORAY!"
everyone cheered.

"Thanks, everyone," Nutkin called.
"Come on, let's play furball!"

"FOOTBALL!"
the players all cried.

"That's what I said,"
Nutkin replied.

The thrilling game went on
until nightfall, and they all had
so much fun that no one quite
remembered to keep score!

THE WOODLAND CUP

Every year we hold the **WOODLAND CUP** to find the best football team. We all join in, but not everyone plays by the rules! Here's a sketch from my dad's journal.

Dug-out
(perfect for bunnies!)

Old Brown
always plays on
the left wing

GO, RABBITS!

GO, RABBITS!

Jeremy Fisher made
a great sliding tackle

Test your TRICK SHOTS and practise your PENALTIES

Peter, Benjamin and Lily used all their football skills to save Nutkin from grumpy Old Brown.

The squirrels showed some pretty fancy footwork too!

Try these football moves to see if you can hop to it like a bunny or shoot like a squirrel striker. First find a ball. (Something bigger than a hazelnut!)

PRACTISE THESE SKILLS WITH A FRIEND:

- "Keepie-uppies" (Keep the ball off the floor using your chest, legs, knees and head.)

- Scoring goals (Take turns to be the goalie.)

- Dribbling the ball as fast as you can.

CONGRATULATIONS!

FOOTBALL SKILLS CERTIFICATE

Awarded to

_____

_____

Age

_____

Peter Rabbit

TEAM CAPTAIN

Peter Rabbit Club

Fantastic football skills.
You're our STAR player!